W9-CKE-157

An Incredible Journey Book

PIRATES

IN PARADISE

by Connie Lee Berry

This book is dedicated to my two amazing boys and their dad. I hope you go to the Caribbean on your nautical adventure and have smooth sailing all the way ~ unlike this deep-water adventure.

ISBN 10: 0977284832
ISBN 13: 9780977284832
This book is part of the Incredible Journey Books series.

Text copyright© 2007 by Connie Lee Berry.
All rights reserved. Published by Kid's Fun Press in 2007.

Printed in the U.S.A.

Table of Contents

Facts About Pirates

~Most pirates lived on ships called schooners or galleys.

~The captain, a strong leader who had the skill and daring to win prize and booty, controlled the ship along with the quartermaster, who was a trusted seaman who knew how to sail. The quartermaster was second-in-command and would distribute rations, gun powder, work, prizes, and punishment.

~Pirates depended mainly on the element of surprise to capture a ship. The pirates would throw grappling hooks onto the other ship and that ship was snagged like a fish on a hook. The pirates would come up from the bow or stern to prevent being shot at by side guns. Pirates usually attacked lightly armed merchant ships because they looked for easy pickings, not an early death.

~Most members of a pirate crew signed a Ship's Articles that stated the division of power and how the booty would be divided.

Pirate Phrases

Shiver Me Timbers-expresses shock or surprise
Bounty-reward in return for something
Booty or **Loot**-treasure or gold taken illegally
Plunder-the act of raiding to rob
Mutiny-to rise against authority
Maroon-to leave stranded on a deserted island
Jolly Roger-a black flag showing white bones and a skull that indicates a pirate ship
Matey-a friend or shipmate
First Mate-the captain's right-hand man
Walk the Plank-a prisoner being forced to walk off a plank of wood into the water
Landlubber or **landlover**-a non-pirate or coward
A merry yarn-a good story
Land ahoy-seeing land
Blow me down-how surprising
Weigh anchor-to haul up the anchor to set sail
Starboard-ship's right-hand side, facing forward
Larboard-ship's left-hand side, facing forward

A Pirate's Life

Even though romanticized, the life of a pirate was harsh. Many obstacles included:

~The smell of the ship: Rotting fish, food, and water (that collected at the bottom of the boat) made the ship reek of foul odor.

~Horrible food and drink: Pirates lived mostly on tack (a hard cracker made up of water, flour, and lard) and dried meat that was so hard it had to be soaked in water before it could be eaten. Water was in short supply, with each pirate getting about a quart of water a day.

~Pesky critters: Some ships had hundreds or even thousands of rats. The ships also housed fleas, poisonous spiders, and scorpions.

~Sleeping quarters: Only the captain had a bunk or bed. The others had to look for a place to sleep, perhaps on a sack of wheat.

~Restrooms: To go to the bathroom, the crew would use holes cut in a board or a sopping bucket in an area called the head at the bow of the ship. Waste went into the sea.

~Boredom: With no entertainment on board, pirates would pass the time singing shanties or songs.

~Danger: Pirates faced the daily possibility of death, being marooned, or being thrown overboard by the crew.

History of Piracy

M ost piracy occurred during the rise and fall of the Spanish colonies in the Americas. As Spain conquered and colonized the Americas, her treasure fleets brought silver, gold, gems, spices, cocoa, and other exotic goods to Spain. This period was from 1520 until the last treasure fleet sailed in 1790.

At the beginning of the 18th century, Spain controlled the Americas and had the strongest navy in the world. Great Britain wanted to gain control, but lacked the resources to build a strong navy. They resorted to privateering. A privateer was an armed ship under papers from a government or a company, called Letters of Marque, to perform specific tasks such as seeking out and attacking the ships of hostile nations. Often the privateers ignored the Marque and did what they pleased. They attacked neutral countries' ships as well as hostile nations but would rarely attack their own country's ships (which would have been treason). The privateers were not paid by the nation or company but by taking spoils from ships they attacked. Unlike pirates, privateers were considered heros by their host nations.

Buccaneers were French settlers in the Caribbean that were known for hunting wild pigs and goats. Many had been French sailors who had jumped ship and settled in the numerous small islands in the Caribbean. As their numbers increased, Spain viewed them as a threat to their New World colonies and laid claim to the islands that they lived on. Spain began a campaign to rid the islands of these vagrants. Because of this, many buccaneers turned to privateering for England to protect British colonies from Spain.

To many, there was no difference between a pirate and a privateer—anyone who robbed at sea was a pirate, and when privateers went beyond the scope of their mission, they became pirates.

In 1713, a treaty was signed in which Spain recognized England's right to colonies in the New World. Great Britain ceased attacks on Spanish ships. After this, English privateering ceased, and many privateers became pirates. No longer were they acting on behalf of the government.

Once governments cracked down on piracy and no longer offered safe harbor, organized piracy began to disappear. Unorganized piracy continued on a much smaller scale.

Piracy Today

Piracy still exists today, although it's generally limited to certain parts of the world, primarily in third-world country territories or in areas with unstable governments.

Today pirates operate in small groups of about a dozen men. They usually travel in unassuming boats such as speed boats or fishing boats that have been stolen.

Their vessels are not usually heavily armed with weapons because it is important for them to go unnoticed by law enforcement or military vessels.

The pirates primarily attack cargo or merchant ships for their goods and sometimes attack when the target ship's crew is not on board to avoid confrontation. They rarely attack private boats.

Prologue

In the first *Incredible Journey Book*, *The Criminal in the Caymans*, two mysterious boxes arrived on Max and Sam's doorstep. In one box, the boys found an old leather journal. Inside the journal was yellowed paper with a note scribbled on the first page that said, "Notes taken wisely can be of great use to you." In the second box, they found a map dated October 11, 1964 and labeled "Max and Sam's Incredible Journey Map."

Since that time, a letter has mysteriously appeared on the map with each trip they take. In the Cayman Islands, a "W" appeared. In Tahiti, an "I" appeared. In Africa, an "S" appeared.

Max and Sam have not discovered who sent the map or the journal or why the letters keep appearing on the map. These mysteries will be solved in a later *Incredible Journey Book*.

Chapter One
The Very Bad Dream

As the moonlight splashed patterns of light into the dark room, a shadow of the bed emerged on the wall. The shadow was still and calm.

All of a sudden, the shadow came alive with activity as it flickered on the wall.

The shadow continued to jump about as Sam, who lay in his bed, thrashed about—flinging his sheet this way and that, as if he were in a ferocious struggle.

Then suddenly, there was a loud plunk . . . and then a groan. . . .

Max woke with a start and screamed, startled by the noise. In the darkness, he could see only specks of light.

The light switch clicked on and brightness filled the room. Mr. Stone rushed over to the bed. "What's wrong?" he said, grabbing Max's shoulders.

Max and his dad saw something move on the floor. They both chuckled with relief when they realized it was Sam.

"That hurt," Sam said, sitting up and rubbing the shoulder he had landed on.

"You have to learn to stay in the bed when you sleep!" his Dad said in a burst of laughter. Mr. Stone's expression grew more serious when he saw Sam's troubled face.

"I had a bad dream," Sam said. "A very, very bad dream."

"What was it about?" Max asked, wondering what could make his brother so worried.

"There were pirates after us—bad ones like

Captain Hook," Sam said, shuddering at the recollection of the cross-eyed, one-toothed pirate who had chased him in his sleep.

"It was just a dream," his dad said, trying to reassure him. "We're all safe—there are no pirates here—unless they're hiding in the closet, of course."

Mr. Stone laughed, trying to lighten Sam's spirits.

Sam still looked troubled. "Can you sleep in here?" he asked his dad.

"There's no room in this bed for the three of us," Mr. Stone said, "and I certainly don't want to sleep on the floor."

The expression on Sam's face worsened.

"Sam, pirates are a thing of the past," his dad said. "You know that."

"They seemed so real," Sam insisted. "It was *so* spooky."

"Come with me," Mr. Stone said, finally giving in. "You can sleep with me. Maybe it's a good thing your mom and Sydney stayed at home."

"This condo *does* seem sort of lonely without them," Sam said.

"Yeah," Max said softly. "I miss Mom and Sydney, too."

The mood in the room was so gloomy that Mr. Stone knew he had better do something to cheer things up.

Like a big overgrown child, he impulsively leaped onto the bed and started jumping up and down. Max, who was still lying in the bed, was tossed all around.

"They don't get to sail around in the Caribbean, but we do!" his dad yelled out obnoxiously as he bounced.

"Yeah!" Sam shouted, jumping up on the bed to join in.

Before long, Max had managed to stand up in-between bounces and join them.

As the clock in the hallway struck midnight, the three of them were still jumping on the bed and laughing boisterously. One by one, they grew tired and collapsed on the bed.

"I've been looking forward to taking you on

this trip for years," Mr. Stone said, trying to catch his breath. "I can't believe the time is finally here."

"Yeah, I remember you talking about it when we were little," Max said.

"Sailing the crystal-blue waters of the Caribbean and charting your own course is one of the greatest experiences you'll ever have," Mr Stone said, grinning. "I'll never forget the trips I took with my dad. The islands that make up the U.S. and the British Virgin Islands are absolutely beautiful, as you can tell from what you've seen so far in St. Thomas."

"Sounds great," Sam mumbled, finally at peace now that the one-eyed pirate had faded from his mind. "I think I'll be okay sleeping in here now."

"All right," his dad said, patting his back. "You know where to find me if you have any more bad dreams."

"Yeah, I know," Sam said, smiling broadly.

Max, who was almost asleep by the time Mr. Stone had turned off the light and left the room, thought about the crystal-blue waters of the ocean. His mind was brought back to their trip to Tahiti and how he had loved to sit on the sand and watch the waves come and go. He remembered the feeling of the sun on his face and being sprayed with sea foam.

Max's eyes flickered open, half expecting to see the bright light of the sun, but instead was greeted with shadowy light. The moonlight had once again flooded the room, projecting shadows on the wall. The stars over the ocean just outside their window were shining brightly, casting a soft glow over the tranquil water.

Before long, the three of them were sound asleep.

Chapter Two
The Strong Survivor

The chirping of birds and the sound of the ocean woke Max and Sam the next morning. Sam got out of bed and stumbled out the open patio door to find Mr. Stone sitting in a lounge chair, reading the newspaper.

"Hello, sleepyhead," he said when he saw Sam. "I thought I'd let you sleep in this morning. You had such a rough night."

"Oh, yeah," Sam said, glancing at his bruised arm and shoulder. "Luckily, the pirates didn't come back again."

"Hopefully they went off to never-never land to live happily ever after," Mr. Stone said with a wink.

"Hopefully," Sam said, grinning.

Max appeared at the door, yawning widely.

"Did you get enough sleep?" his dad asked him.

"Yeah," Max mumbled as he went over to the edge of the patio to look out on the sea.

Max took a deep breath and inhaled the fresh, salty air. He watched as the waves crashed on the beach.

"We're going to grab some breakfast and get going," Mr. Stone said. "I'm anxious to get to the marina to rent our boat."

An hour later, after they had eaten and carried their luggage down to the lobby, the Stone family waited outside on a bench by the curb.

Sam looked around at the beautiful plants that surrounded them. Large pots, overflowing with cheerful yellow and purple flowers, lined the walkway to the curb. A group of leafy plants boasting bright-red blossoms were planted in a bed by the bench. Cages of exotic birds were scattered in the tropical foliage, making the area sound more like a jungle than a waiting area.

Sam took a path to one of the cages that housed a beautiful blue and gold macaw parrot. He had always had a fascination with these large, clever birds.

"Hello," Sam said, staring at his green-crested head.

"Hel-lo," the parrot echoed back.

"Sam," Mr. Stone called out. "Our shuttle is here."

"Bye-bye," Sam said to the parrot.

"Bye-bye," the parrot repeated back.

Sam smiled at the parrot. He then ran back along the path and climbed on the shuttle bus marked "Bareboat Yacht Rental." He grinned excitedly at Max and his dad.

As the vehicle zigzagged through the rocky countryside, Max gasped every time they passed another car. The roads were so narrow that the cars barely scraped past each other.

To make it even worse, the cars are driven in the left lane in the Virgin Islands. Max and Sam kept forgetting this and crying out, thinking their vehicle was on the wrong side of the road.

After fifteen long minutes and many harrowing close calls, the shuttle bus pulled in front of a white, rusted building and stopped. Max and Sam could see scores of sailboats lining both sides of a long, wooden dock.

They grabbed their bags and ran off the bus toward the line of beautiful boats. They paraded up and down the gangplank in front of the boats trying to guess which one was theirs.

"Maybe it's this one," Sam called out, staring at a boat named *Caribbean Queen*.

"I think it's this one," Max shouted out as he ran in front of a boat called *Jewel of the Sea*.

"No, I want it to be this one," Sam said stubbornly, planting himself in front of his boat of choice. He stared down at the water shimmering below the dock—it twinkled in the sunlight.

The boys stood in front of their favorite

boats for a few minutes until their dad came out of the rental office and started down the dock. He glanced down at his rental paperwork that had "Boat Slip 13" marked in bold letters at the top.

With Max and Sam following behind him, Mr. Stone walked down the long bridge, staring down at the numbers painted on its sides. When he got to "13" he stopped.

All three of them stared at the boat in this

slip and read the boat's name.

"*The Strong Survivor*," Mr. Stone mumbled.

"Survivor of *what*?" Max shrieked.

"Arrrgh, ye landlubbers," Mr. Stone creaked in a drawling pirate voice. "Ye lads climb aboard and stow yer sea chests like good li'l swabbies while I tally the grub in the larder. Then we'll weigh anchor. Savvy?"

"Aye-Aye, Captain," Sam said, saluting him.

Chapter Three
The Lost Soul

After a nerve-racking trek through the tight quarters of the marina, an exhausted Max and Sam lay sprawled out on the white, freshly mopped deck. They loved the feeling of the sun beaming down on them, showering them with warmth. Luckily for them, a steady breeze whipped by, cooling them off like a natural fan.

It was so serene out on the open sea. The only noise that could be heard was the flapping of the sails above them.

Mr. Stone relaxed as he stood at the wheel and stared at the endless sea of blue. He had worked furiously before they had left the marina storing their food rations, checking weather charts, and plotting their course.

After a while, Max and Sam got up and sat on the built-in benches by the instrument panel to get a better view. They watched as a group of seagulls flew gracefully overhead.

Sam's eyes followed them across the sky,

until he thought he spotted a boat in the distance.

"Sail ho!" Sam shouted, continuing his stint as a pirate. "I see a sail over the horizon."

Max rolled his eyes. "Well, shiver me timbers," he mumbled sarcastically.

The gentle rocking of the boat had put Max in a relaxed state, and at that moment, he didn't care if there was a fleet of boats approaching.

Sam was curious. He hurried below the deck to get the binoculars. When he came back a couple of minutes later, he strained his eyes to find the tiny object again.

Sam worked at adjusting the binoculars to get a clear focus. Finally, he had the object in plain sight. . . .

Sam stared at a rusty, old sailboat that looked like it had been out to sea for years. He noticed some faint lettering on the side of the boat. It looked like the words had been painted over, but some letters managed to peek through.

He ran down below once again to find paper and a pen.

When he came back, he picked up the binoc-ulars. He carefully studied each letter on the side of the boat, writing it down on paper as he recognized it. A couple of letters were too vague to decipher. After a few minutes, he stared at what he had written.

T h e   L st   S o l

He looked at the letters over and over again, his eyes racing past them. . . . Then it hit him. He filled in the missing letters to form the words "The Lost Soul."

"Dad!" Sam called over to Mr. Stone. "The boat's name over there is *The Lost Soul*."

"*What*?" his dad answered, visibly shaken. "It couldn't be!"

His dad abandoned the wheel of the boat and scurried over to where Sam was standing. He grabbed the binoculars. "I don't see any name on the boat," he said after a few moments of careful examination.

"The letters are faint, but they're there," Sam insisted, grabbing the binoculars back. He studied the boat for a few minutes and then set the binoculars down. "The boat must have turned so that we can't see the letters now," he said.

"Why can't the boat be called *The Lost Soul*?" Max asked, puzzled.

"Because *that* boat has been missing for three years!" Mr. Stone responded. "The boat was stolen and its owners marooned on an island. Thankfully, the owners were rescued after a couple of days—they claimed modern-day pirates had stolen their boat."

"*Pirates*?" Max shrieked. "You told us pirates don't exist anymore."

"I meant the ones like in the past, with a patch over their eye and wearing a hook for a hand," Mr. Stone said. "Unfortunately, there are still men who rob at sea and are considered pirates."

"How do you know so much about *The Lost Soul*?" Sam blurted out.

There was silence for a few seconds . . . and

then Mr. Stone said, "Because I remember reading about it, that's why."

Their dad glanced over at the mysterious boat in the distance. He was glad to see it was heading in the opposite direction.

"Let's go snorkeling," Mr. Stone suddenly suggested, walking back over to the wheel. "Get your bathing suits on. We're about thirty minutes away from a fantastic reef just off a small island."

Max smiled at the thought of relaxing in the sparkling water. He jumped up to follow Sam down the ladder to get changed. But before he did, something made him turn back around to study the old boat in the distance. He picked up the binoculars and stared at the object through the lenses to make sure it was still drifting away from them. . . .

By now, the boat was just a speck in the sea, getting smaller by the minute. In a few minutes, it would disappear.

Out of sight, out of mind, Max tried to convince himself.

Chapter Four
Danger Zone

An hour later, *The Strong Survivor* was anchored beside a protected harbor filled with the most abundant fish they had ever seen. Max and Sam were dazzled by the brightly colored schools of fish that seemed to be everywhere under the tranquil, blue waters surrounding the uninhabited island.

Max pretended to be one of the fish as he glided along in the crystal-clear water. He floated effortlessly along, following different groups of fish. He was in perfect harmony with these amazing fish—they didn't even seem to notice he was there. Mr. Stone explained to Max—in-between bouts of getting water in their snorkel tubes and coming up for air—that the fish weren't threatened by humans because there weren't many fishermen around.

Max noticed sand being churned up on the ocean floor. He watched as a stingray emerged from its hiding place and skirted across the sand, its long tail extending from its back. The

stingray's body was thin, making it very easy to bury itself and go undetected.

Max watched this odd, wafer-looking sea animal for several minutes. He thought it strange that its eyes were on the top of its body, making it seem impossible for the poor animal to see where it was going.

Meanwhile, Sam was having a great time staring at a jellyfish floating in front of him. He almost swam past it without noticing its see-through, glob-like body. Luckily, he noticed its dangling brown tentacles and managed to stay far away from them so he wouldn't get stung.

He had always heard that a jellyfish's sting can be extremely painful and remembered that his cousin Lindsay from Kentucky was stung by one. Her wound got infected, leaving her in agony for days.

All of a sudden, Max tensed up and poked his head above water. Sam could hear his brother trying to say something, but with a snorkel in his mouth, the words ended up sounding more like a panicky gurgling noise.

Sam sensed that he'd better find out what Max was trying to say, and he stuck his head up.

Max finally took the snorkel tube from his mouth and coughed up some water, still desperately trying to get his words out. "Bar-ra-cu-da," he managed to say in-between coughs. He pointed to a nearby cave in the reef.

"Dad!" Sam yelled to his dad who was farther out in the ocean. "Barracuda."

Max and Sam didn't know whether to swim away or freeze. Their dad had told them that it was important not to act like you are in distress in the water. He said that jerky movements make you look like easy prey to ocean predators.

Sam tread water next to Max. It took every bit of courage they had not to scream and scramble away as fast as they could. But the last thing they wanted to do was go fluttering through the water like frightened prey.

As the minutes ticked by, the only thing that kept them from succumbing to their fear was the sight of their dad swimming toward them.

When Mr. Stone reached them, he grabbed their hands and slowly pulled each one of them to his side. The three of them slowly swam away.

After they had gotten a safe distance away, Mr. Stone stopped and came up to the surface. Max and Sam poked their faces above water to see what he was doing.

Mr. Stone tried to ease their fear, as he bobbed around in the water. "Don't worry, barracudas *rarely* attack people," he said. "They do so only in murky water when they mistake a human for a fish. And even if they *do* bite you, they will quickly realize their mistake because of the taste and swim away. They like the taste of *fish*, not people."

Feeling a little bit comforted, Max and Sam's curiosity got the best of them, and they stuck their heads under water to catch a glimpse of the six-foot-long fish. Through the clear water, they could see not one barracuda—but three—hovering around the reef.

Their long, slender bodies looked harmless

enough—that is until you noticed their fierce-looking heads with the bottom jaw jutting out, exposing razor-sharp teeth.

Sam stared at one of the beasts. He thought the unusual fish looked like a submarine with an angry head, fins, and a tail stuck on. He shuddered at the sight of its long, sharp teeth, feeling sorry for any fish that crossed paths with such a frightful predator.

Mr. Stone nudged them under water and pointed to a colorful wall. Within seconds, a green moray eel poked his head out of a hole in the coral.

The eel's body soon came out of its crevice and Max and Sam could see how long and muscular it was—it looked more like a forbidding sea serpent than anything else. The only thing that resembled a fish was a long, continuous fin that went from its head to its tail.

The haunting sea animal looked like a monster from a scary lagoon. It swayed its long, scaleless body back and forth in the midst of wild seagrass, eerily opening and closing its mouth as its round eyes stared blankly into space. Every time the eel opened its mouth, Max and Sam flinched at the sight of its jagged, pointed teeth.

After Max had watched the erratic movements of the eel for a few minutes, he grew nervous about viewing this strange underwater world and longed for the normalness of the boat. He was anxious to get out of the highly active waters, worried about what other kind of sea life might be lurking around.

Max swam to the surface. "Let's get back to the boat," he managed to huff out with his breathing tube still in his mouth.

Sam and Mr. Stone poked their heads above the water to see what Max was saying.

"Huh?" Sam said, thinking Max sounded like he was speaking gibberish.

Max was getting impatient. He didn't want to take the time to remove the tube from his mouth—he wanted to get back to the boat as fast as he could. He vigorously pointed at the boat and then started swimming toward it.

Sam and Mr. Stone followed.

Swimming as fast as he could, Max thought about how the ocean didn't seem much different than the jungles of Africa with danger lurking around every corner—same game but different predators. In both cases, fear was widespread.

Chapter Five
Starry Night

It was nine o'clock at night, and the moon cast a soft glow on the dark, deep water. Thousands of twinkling stars shimmered in the sky above.

Max looked up from his book and peered around. It was an eerie feeling, being out in the middle of the sea. The only sign of other humans being around was the distant lights from their boats.

Max's mind flooded with thoughts about the

mysterious sailboat with the painted-over let-ters, wondering if one of the boats in the dis-tance could be it.

Max shivered. A boat being stolen by *pirates* and its owners being marooned on an island? It seemed like a plot right out of an adventure novel.

The Lost Soul was a pretty spooky name for a boat. Max hoped his brother was wrong about what the letters on the boat spelled out.

Max stared out at the sea in the darkness. It was sort of lonely sailing off the beaten path, as their dad called it. Mr. Stone said he liked to visit the less crowded islands—many were just as beautiful as the well-known ones.

Max looked over at his dad, still reading his book. The pages seemed to glow as the reading lamp splashed light upon them.

Max looked over at Sam, still reading his comic book. He could see the shadow of his brother's face smiling off and on as the words on the pages amused him. Once in a while, he would hear Sam chuckle out loud.

Max suddenly remembered his notes from their first sailing lesson after dinner. He put his book on the table and picked up his notes. He read:

Eels-They lie in wait for prey to come to them.

Barracudas-They are known to follow snorkelers and swimmers. Since they usually don't attack humans, it is thought that barracudas view humans as large predators and want to scavenge their left-over prey.

Stingrays-They can't see prey since their eyes are on top. They rely on smell to find food.

Sharks-Reefs form a natural barrier to protect snorkelers from sharks. Shark attacks are very rare.

Green buoy-It should be on the sailboat's right as it goes out the channel. The channel marks a safe, deep-water passage in the sea. On the way back, green should be on the left.

Red buoy-It should be on the sailboat's left out the channel, on the right going back.

Once Sam finished reading his comic book, he closed it and set it on the table. He glanced over at his dad and Max, their reading material aglow. He was thinking about what he could do next when he suddenly remembered something.

He hurried down below and got out the old leather journal from his suitcase. As he held it in his hands, he looked down at it. Lifeless and dull with age, he wondered why it meant so much to him.

He thought back to their trip to the Cayman Islands and to the first time he had written in the journal's worn, yellowed pages. He smiled when he remembered writing down their plan to capture the criminal.

Sam was just about to open the old leather journal when his dad's voice interrupted him.

"Sam," Mr. Stone called out. "What are you doing down there? Don't tell me you're sea-sick."

"I'm not," Sam assured him. "I'll be right up."

As soon as Sam had climbed up the ladder

and onto the deck, a cool gust of wind caught him off guard. He stumbled and dropped the journal. It tumbled through the darkness.

Sam cried out in distress. He had grown so attached to the old thing that he couldn't imagine going on trips without it.

He fell to his knees and patted the hard, worn deck but couldn't find it.

"Help!" Sam called out, beginning to panic. "I've lost it."

"Huh?" Max said, looking up from his notes. "What have you lost?"

"The journal," Sam cried out. "It's disappeared."

Max put his notes down and ran over to Sam. He crouched beside him and shined his reading light on the floor, pausing a few seconds in each spot.

"It's gone!" Max wailed. "It's disappeared."

Mr. Stone hurried over with a flashlight he had retrieved from a bin. He moved it across the floor.

"I told you—it's lost," Sam said sadly.

"It couldn't have just disappeared," Mr. Stone said. "Is there a chance it could have gone overboard?"

Max shrieked at the thought of their treasured journal plummeting to the bottom of the ocean floor, gone just as fast as it had appeared on their doorstep.

"Wait a minute," Mr. Stone said, catching a glimpse of some paper on the floor underneath the table. He shined the light on the spot to take a closer look. The three of them dove down to the spot at the same time.

"The map," Sam said, scooping up a piece of the map with his hand. His dad shined the light on it for the three of them to get a better look.

"It doesn't look damaged," Max said, cheering up a bit. "Thank goodness it didn't get wet."

The three of them knelt down on the floor, staring at the section of the map. It looked especially old in the spotlight. Its frayed edges looked fragile and worn.

As Sam stared down at the section of the

map, his eyes shifted to the "W" by the initials for the Cayman Islands. He then found the "I" by Tahiti. Sam tried to find the "S" above Africa but soon realized that the continent was on the other section of the map.

Sam searched for the "V. I." their dad had written on the map during the plane ride there to mark the location of the Virgin Islands.

As he stared down at the map, he suddenly got chills. . . . There was a "D" written above the Virgin Islands. Sam looked over at Max.

Max must have spotted it, too. He had turned pale and his eyes bulged, his face fixed on the map.

Mr. Stone brushed against Sam's arm on his way up. "What's wrong, son?" he said. "You have goose bumps on your skin."

Sam was just about to tell Mr. Stone about the strange letters appearing on the map when his dad started scanning the deck for the missing journal. He walked around slowly, shining the light in every corner of the deck.

"It has to be here somewhere," Mr. Stone

mumbled. "Unless the piece of the map fell out of the journal before it went overboard."

Sam was too preoccupied to hear what his dad was saying—his thoughts swirled with uncertainty.

He debated whether to tell his dad about the mysterious letters on the map. In a strange way, he was scared that if he told someone other than Max, the letters would stop appearing. And as puzzling as the letters appearing were, it was exciting as well.

Max bumped into Sam and brought him reeling back to reality. Max had recovered from his shock and was crawling around under the table feeling for the journal. All at once, there was a thud.

Max groaned. "Ouch," he said, rubbing the top of his head. "That hurt."

Mr. Stone abruptly threw his hands up in the air. "Let's go to bed," he said, frustrated. "We're exhausted, and it's hard to find anything on this dark boat."

Max and Sam started to protest, thinking

they'd rather stay up all night than go to bed with the journal lost, possibly at sea.

Max thought back to the night they had discovered the journal and how he had stayed up most of the night trying to figure out where it had come from. And now they had lost it—even before they found out the truth about its origin.

"Come on, guys," Mr. Stone insisted. "We'll be able to see better in the morning light."

As the boys followed their dad down to the cabin, they felt like they had lost the most valuable thing in the world. At that moment, they would have gladly traded the most brilliant diamond or a pot of gold for a glimpse of that old, dusty journal again.

And to think their prized possession might be sleeping with the sharks on the deep ocean floor, never to be seen again.

"Why did you have to bring the journal to the deck?" Max snapped at Sam, casting blame.

Sam's spirits sank even lower. "I just wanted to look at the map," he murmured. "Sorry."

Max knew how lousy Sam felt. "Maybe we'll find it in the morning," he said, his voice trying to sound optimistic.

Inside, though, both of them thought they'd never see the journal again.

Chapter Six
The Sunrise

S am couldn't stand the noise anymore. He sat up in the stuffy, small quarters and looked at the clock. It read five o'clock.

"Max!" he cried out, trying to wake him up. "You're having a bad dream."

It didn't do much to rouse him from his sleep. Max continued to toss his body from side to side. He cried out, "No!"

Sam got up and felt his way to the galley in the darkness. The only light came from a couple of night-lights in the cabin. He opened the refrigerator chest and felt around until he found a bottle of water.

Sam stumbled back to his sleeping brother with the bottle in his hand. Max was still in anguish, slinging his arms around. Sam knew what he needed to do—he twisted off the cap and poured some of the chilly water from the bottle on his brother's face.

Max shot up from the bed, looking stunned.

Sam crouched on the floor, knowing that his brother would be fighting mad when he discovered what he had done.

Oddly, Max didn't yell or show any sign of anger. He just sat there with water dripping from his chin. Sam could see his face from the glow from one of the night-lights.

Sam stayed silent. He didn't know what to expect next.

Max finally spoke. "It seemed so real. There was a pirate laughing . . . a pirate, just like in your dream. But the laugh terrified me."

"It's probably because we're in a boat, out in

the middle of nowhere," Sam explained away the coincidence of their dreams. "It didn't help that I spotted that boat in the distance called—"

"Don't say its name," Max said, shuddering, partly from being scared and partly from being drenched with cold water.

"Yeah, I was probably getting spooked by that boat," Max continued. "Pirates like that one don't really exist these days."

"Yeah," Sam said, trying to make himself believe it. "They're a thing of the past."

"What are you boys doing up?" they heard a voice say, as a dark figure emerged.

They both jumped and looked up to see their dad standing in the doorway. "Your talking woke me up," Mr. Stone said, yawning.

"I had a bad dream," Max said.

"Don't tell me Captain Hook came to see you, too," their dad said.

Wanting to forget about his dream, Max shook his head.

"Since we're all awake, I've got an idea," Mr. Stone said. "We can watch the sun rise."

The thought of daylight made Max and Sam smile. Everything was less scary in the light.

Mr. Stone flicked on the cabin lights and the small area came alive with brightness.

"Let's go," Max said, cheering up. He dashed through the cabin and up the stairs to the deck, while Sam and his dad followed close behind.

Max took a seat on the bench and stared up at the black sky dotted with tiny stars. He looked out at the water, still as dark as ever.

Mr. Stone plopped down beside him. "Do you know which way we should face to watch the sun rise?" he asked.

"I know," Max said, "the east."

"And where's the east?" Mr. Stone said.

Max hesitated a moment and then remembered the compass on the instrument panel. He got up and ran over to it. Even with the deck light on, it was still too dark to make out the tiny letters on the dial.

Sam caught on to what he was doing and handed him the reading light from his book, still lying on the table.

Max shined it on the compass and found the "E" for east. "It's over there," Max said, pointing across the sky.

Mr. Stone sounded pleased. "Great job," he said.

As the three of them faced east, they talked about their plans for the day.

"I know a beautiful area called The Baths we could visit today," Mr. Stone said. "You don't see many places like this."

"What's it like?" Sam asked, thinking it must be pretty special to impress their dad, who had been to so many places.

"You'll see," Mr. Stone said, grinning ever so slightly. "Once daylight breaks, we'll pull the anchor up and head that way. It should only take a couple of hours from here. It's on Virgin Gorda, one of the British Virgin Islands."

Max and Sam smiled knowing the wind would soon be blowing through their hair and the sails flapping above them. It felt so soothing to be gliding along in the ocean with the sun beaming down on them. It was the calmest feeling in the world.

Without the boys even realizing it, the sky had changed colors and the light had gone from black to dim. The boys knew that at any moment the sun would peek its head up to signal the start of a new day.

Sam looked over at the eastern horizon, determined not to miss the first glance of the sun. When he did, he thought he caught sight of a boat across the way. It was hard to tell for sure because the growing light was still so dim.

Sam could hardly focus on the sun as it finally rose above the horizon. He was focused on the tiny object across the water.

Sam stared at the small speck he thought was a boat. He nervously wondered if it could be *The Lost Soul*.

The speck was there one minute and gone the next. Whatever it was had faded into the distance.

Reflections bouncing off the water can do weird things to your vision, Sam decided.

Chapter Seven
A Scene From the Past

M ax and Sam were seated on the deck getting ready to set sail when their dad called up to them from below.

"Come here, guys. You're going to want to see this," Mr. Stone said, his voice sounding distant even though it came from the cabin right below them.

The boys rushed down to where their dad had been all morning long, sitting at the table mapping out their trip and studying the weather forecast.

"What do you want us to see?" Sam asked.

"Look over there—in the corner by the stairs," he said, nodding his head.

At first, the boys didn't see anything. The brown wood on the floor camouflaged the object until they moved closer.

"The journal!" Sam cried out when he spotted it. "How did it get *there*?"

"Instead of falling overboard, it must have fallen down the open hatch and landed there," Mr. Stone said, wondering why they hadn't thought of the possibility the night before.

"I can't believe it," Max said, smiling giddily. "It was right under our nose the whole time."

"Yeah, as we slept, it was right outside our door," Sam said, his eyes twinkling with happiness.

"Let's keep the journal down here, tucked far away from the water," Max insisted.

"I'll put it back in my suitcase right now," Sam said, relieved to have another chance to take care of the precious journal.

Mr. Stone looked content. "You better," he said. "I don't think a journal like that one comes along every day." He closed his chart book and grinned. "The weather is going to be perfect today, not a cloud or storm projected anywhere along our course."

Sam smiled back at him. "Looks like it's going to be a good day. Wait for me to help with the anchor."

Mr. Stone waited for Sam to come back before all three of them headed up.

When they got to the deck, Max and Sam watched as their dad jumped into the crystal-clear, warm water to refresh himself before they started their journey to Virgin Gorda. The water was so clear they could see him gliding along under the surface, following a green sea turtle. After he trailed it for a few moments, Mr. Stone shot up from the water and inhaled the fresh air.

"Heave in the anchor, boys," Mr. Stone instructed them, treading water in the calm sea.

Max and Sam hurried over to the anchor line

at the bow of the boat. They took turns crank-ing the wheel to wind the rope up. It took all of their strength to turn the handle of the windlass.

Max smiled at their progress. He could now see the heavy, metal anchor coming out of the water, trailing along at the end of the chain.

"Good job," Mr. Stone yelled, climbing over the railing and onto the boat. "Look, the anchor is almost here."

Sweat streamed down Sam's face and into his eyes. Sam stayed strong, resisting the urge to abandon his grip and wipe the sweat away.

Sam's determination paid off. He pulled the last few feet of chain in, and the anchor settled into its position on the roller.

Max locked it in place just as his dad had instructed him to do the day before.

"Sailing is hard work," Sam said, panting. "I wouldn't want to do it alone."

"That's why it's better to travel with a first mate," their dad said. "Or in this case, *two* first mateys."

The mere mention of a pirate's word made

Mr. Stone go into a frenzy. He began to jump excitedly around the bow of the boat like he was in a sword fight, slashing his invisible blade in the air.

After one final blow of his sword, their dad stopped moving. He squinched up his face and covered one eye. "Well, blow me down, me li'l hearties," his voice creaked. "Ye weighed anchor like ye was an old salt. Ye make an old seadog like me so proud." Mr. Stone put his hand on his heart and sighed.

Max and Sam giggled at their dad's dramatic pirate show. He had a vivid imagination.

As the boat began to drift, Mr. Stone made his way to the stern to take the wheel. Max and Sam followed and took seats next to him on the bench. It felt nice to relax after working up a sweat hauling up the anchor.

Max moved over to the other bench and stretched out. He cupped his hands beneath his head to form a cushion against the hard fiberglass surface of the built-in bench. He looked over to his side and stared up at the clear, blue sky. Dad was right about the weather, he thought. There were no clouds in sight.

The boat gently rocked. Max felt relaxed now that they were on their way. It wasn't long until the motion of the boat had put him to sleep. . . .

Max woke up two hours later to the sound of his brother yelling.

"Is this the place?" Sam called out to his dad, amazed at the sight of so many boats in one place.

"So this is where most of the boats have been hanging out," Max said groggily, rising up from the bench and smiling at the sight of so much activity.

Max slowly grabbed the binoculars off of the table to get a closer view. He gave Sam a minute-by-minute update of what he saw. "I see a lady with a little girl wading through the most bluish-green water I have ever seen. . . . A man just jumped off a boat. He appears to be swimming to shore. . . . Wow, would you look at that yacht! It's gigantic."

"Oh, let me see *those*," Sam said, coming over to snatch the binoculars away from Max. He stood silent for a few moments as he studied the blur of activity through the lenses.

"It looks like a scene out of a dinosaur movie," Sam gasped, as he stared at huge boulders and caves. It felt like they were being led into the past. The landscape seemed so unspoiled and untouched—yet there were so many people around.

Sam decided that it looked more like a set of a movie than a real place—it was too picturesque and beautiful to be real.

Mr. Stone let out a gasp as they drew near. "It's just like I remembered," he said, taken back by the island's beauty. He inhaled the fresh, salty air surrounding the tranquil place.

"Let's anchor over there by that cove," Mr. Stone said. "It should be deep enough water."

Mr. Stone kept a watchful eye on the water depth gauge as their boat glided through the water, passing several boats along the way. Finally, Mr. Stone gently steered the boat's wheel starboard to ease into the cove.

Max looked over at his dad and recognized the same slightly tense look that had come over his dad's face the last time they had anchored.

Mr. Stone jumped up and raced toward the anchor line. He quickly pulled out chain and rope from the anchor rope locker. He unhooked the pin from the anchor and gently lowered it to the water, feeding down chain and then rope until the anchor was fifty feet under water. He then tied off the line.

Their dad ran back to the controls and threw the boat in reverse. He gunned the engine.

The engine roared as it tried to pull the boat backward, but the sailboat stayed put. Mr. Stone smiled. It had worked—the anchor had dug into the sandy bottom and had taken hold.

Max fixed his eyes on a swaying palm tree on the nearby beach. Its long branches swung back and forth as its tall, thin trunk shot up to the clear, blue sky. He let out a sigh. It was going to be a beautiful day.

Chapter Eight
The Baths

As Max, Sam, and their dad swam through the warm water toward the beach, they looked around in disbelief.

Even the water in this place looked staged. Its bluish-green color was so vivid it looked as though someone had poured barrels of food coloring into the sparkling water.

The island's towering boulders were scattered about and glistened as the warm sun beamed down upon them. The rock formations created endless coves with natural pools.

"This place is incredible," Max said, wading into one of the pools. He looked down and was startled to see schools of fish swimming around. The water was so transparent that a mask and snorkel weren't needed to view the underwater life.

"Yeah, I didn't know places like this existed," Sam said, looking around at the many caves, clearings, and paths. "Where do the paths lead?" he asked.

"They lead to places like this," Mr. Stone answered. "This place is teeming with naturally formed pools. You couldn't create a place like this even if you tried."

Max and Sam nodded their heads to agree.

"There is an old copper mine somewhere on this island. It has stone buildings and a mine shaft," Mr. Stone said. "I hiked to it the last time I was here, with my parents. I was in college back then."

"That must have been a long time ago," Max said.

"Hey, what do you mean?" Mr. Stone said. "I'm not *that* old."

"You're not that young either," Sam said, teasing his dad.

"Are there sharks around here?" Max asked.

"You'll find sharks in most areas of the Caribbean ocean," Mr. Stone said. "But they usually leave you alone. I've crossed paths with many sharks when snorkeling. You'll be happy to know that there have been very few shark attacks in the Virgin Islands."

"A *few* is way too many," Sam said, worried.

"Sharks are like barracudas. They usually attack people when they mistake them for a fish," their dad explained. "That's why you shouldn't wear glittery things in the water like jewelry because sharks and other sea creatures will mistake the shine for scales of a fish."

A few minutes later, the three of them were stretched out in the white, powdery sand. The beach was in an inlet so that the rocks surrounding it blocked the harsh rays of the sun, allowing only soft indirect light to filter in. The boulders formed a barrier between the ocean's waves.

The only sounds that could be heard were the waves lapping on the other side of the rock wall and the occasional chatter of other tourists walking by.

After a while, Max got up to stretch his legs. He walked around the cove to the wide open view of the sea. Many boats had left by now—only two other boats remained besides theirs.

Max thought he saw a shark's fin circling one of the boats. He trembled at the thought of having to swim back to their boat. He wished they had taken their small dinghy to shore.

Just as he turned to go back to the cove, he saw a glimmer of another boat across the ripples of water. It had faint letters on its side. Max gulped hard. . . . Could *The Lost Soul* be following them?

Chapter Nine
Sounds in the Night

The Stone family was exhausted after a sun-drenched afternoon of swimming and hiking along the slippery rock paths. Luckily, they had managed to swim to their boat unscathed by a shark, and the boat with the faded letters had vanished once again.

All was well when they settled down for a good night's rest at around ten o'clock. The stars had once again taken their place in the sky and did their best to cast light on the dark

Caribbean water.

The aroma of the sea wafted into the cabin from the open hatch. Max and Sam had grown to like the smell of the sea. In an odd way, it smelled comforting and fresh.

It was three o'clock in the morning when Sam started tossing and turning. In his sleep, he could hear voices say, "Take him to the other boat!"

"My pleasure," he heard a raspy voice reply.

Then he heard Max's voice say, "Sam, wake up. Please wake up."

Sam mumbled in his sleep, "Max, this is just a dream. It's not real."

Max began to shake Sam, desperate for him to snap out of his dream-like state. "This time it *is* real. . . . You have to wake up."

Sam's eyes opened slowly to find Max weeping at his side. Everything was foggy in his mind, and the cabin was dark.

Max pinched him hard. "Snap out of it. There are people on the boat, and they're taking Dad somewhere!"

Max paused for a moment and then added, "They're not going to take him without a fight!"

With those words, Max suddenly got a burst of courage and stumbled through the small cabin. Max was filled with more rage and fear than he had ever felt before, and he shook uncontrollably.

Sam, wide awake now, panicked at the thought of being left alone on the ship without Max or his dad. "I'm coming, too," he sobbed as he made his way through the darkness.

When Max and Sam reached the deck, it was lit up, and they could see their dad surrounded by several gruff men. They gasped at the sight of their dad's feet and hands bound with rope and his mouth taped shut.

When Mr. Stone saw them, his eyes were filled with anguish. He tried desperately to speak, but he only managed to grunt through the tape.

Max yelled with all his might at the two filthy, bearded men who held their dad by his arms. "Let him go!" he bellowed out.

Rattled by the unexpected determination coming from such a small boy, the grungy men were taken off guard. Their dad slipped from their grip and fell to the floor. Mr. Stone tried to crawl away but found it impossible because of the tight rope around his ankles.

"You're not getting away that easy," one of the men said nastily. "You're going on that boat whether you like it or not."

Two other men swept Mr. Stone up by his arms and legs, swinging him back and forth like a hammock. "One, two, three, four—"

On the count of four, they tossed the boys' dad over the railing. His body flew across the air and landed with a loud thump onto the deck of another boat that was tied up to theirs.

"Dad!" Max cried out with tears streaming down his face. "Are you okay?"

The boat was so close to theirs that Max could almost reach out and touch it.

Sam immediately recognized the old, rusty boat he had spotted on their first day at sea. "The Lost Soul," he mouthed in astonishment.

Max and Sam had the same thought. They both tried to climb onto the railing so they could jump to the other boat. All they could think about was getting to their dad.

Two men scooped them up in their arms, as the boys fought furiously to get free.

"It's no use," one of the men said, smiling wickedly. "We've got you now."

"Let us go!" Max screamed. "Let us go with our dad!"

"Sorry, boys. It might be nice to have a couple of you around to get us cold drinks and cook our grub," the biggest man hackled. "We might even need a couple of little hostages if it comes down to it."

"Please," Sam cried out. "Please let us go."

"Don't get so upset," a tall man said with a tear in his eye. "We'll let you go when we get to port."

"What are you, a softy?" the biggest and seemingly most wicked man teased his comrade.

Max and Sam knew there was nothing they

could do. The men quickly hauled up the anchor, cast off the lines connecting their boat to *The Lost Soul*, and raised the sails. The boat slowly sailed away from their dad. . . . He was all alone in the darkness aboard *The Lost Soul* adrift at sea.

Tears streamed down the boys' faces as they stared out onto the black sea. The rusty, old boat was becoming farther and farther away with each passing minute.

As devastated as Max and Sam were, the unsavory men were equally as joyful. They were thrilled their plan had worked.

After traveling in the darkness for a while, Max and Sam could hear the raspy voice of one of the men. "It's great to sail in such a nice boat as this one," the man marveled. "The other boat was so old it was falling apart."

"In the morning, we'll head to Puerto Rico to have it painted," another man said. "Who knows—maybe we'll sail around in it awhile before selling it, but we really need some cash. Let's get some shut-eye now."

Chapter Ten
Tea at Midnight

The next day, Max and Sam sat motionless at the side of the boat, still in a state of shock. They had been like that for hours, sitting side by side and staring out onto the sea, hoping to get a glimpse of *The Lost Soul*.

One of the pirates walked up. "You better eat some grub or you'll get sick," his coarse voice bellowed out, as he crammed bread into his mouth. He grabbed Max and Sam by the arms and dragged them across the deck. He forced each of them to go down the ladder and into the cabin.

The boys collapsed into a corner by the ladder, where they had found the old leather journal just the day before. It seemed so long ago now.

The tall pirate who had shown a little bit of kindness to them the day before walked over and handed each of them a piece of bread. Max and Sam took the bread, but instead of eating it, let the pieces fall to the floor.

The other pirates ignored them and shoveled as much food as they could into their mouths, acting as if they hadn't eaten in days.

They had made a feast from abundant food they had found in the food chest. The normally deprived men had hit the jackpot—the locker was filled with all kinds of vegetables, meats, and breads—all of which Mr. Stone had provisioned for their family trip.

After finally getting full, one looked up at Max and Sam's blank stares. He snarled at them. "What's wrong with you? Haven't you ever seen anyone eat before?"

Max and Sam didn't respond. They sat there, numb inside. They had lost their dad, and nothing else mattered.

After dinner, the men's laughter and story-telling roared from above while Max and Sam sat silently down below. Their heartbreak was unimaginable.

As the sun sank below the horizon and the cabin fell dark, Max and Sam drifted off to sleep, trying to escape the hopelessness of their situation. . . .

A few hours later, Max woke to a chirping sound in his ear. At first, he didn't remember what had happened and why he was asleep on the floor. He stared curiously at the dark outline of a bird that had mysteriously found its way through the open hatch and down into the cabin. The bird stared at Max for a brief moment and then flew back through the open hatch.

"I'm awake now. Are you happy?" he mumbled. He almost felt like his old self again until he suddenly remembered, and the reality came plummeting back to him.

"Get up!" Max whispered, nudging his brother who was still asleep on the floor. "I need your help."

Sam sat up, dazed and confused. He stared across the dark cabin at the lit-up clock on a shelf that read 11:00.

"I have a feeling everything is going to be okay," Max said calmly. He smiled and said, "A little bird told me so."

"*What*?" Sam said angrily. "How could anything possibly get better? We can't jump off this boat and swim to Dad. We're probably miles and miles away from him by now."

"Yeah, you're right," Max admitted. "We're sort of stuck on this boat for now. But if we think hard enough, I know we can figure out what to do."

Max and Sam both flinched when they heard footsteps up above. The pirates were still awake and going strong.

Max whispered, "Let's pretend we're still asleep. Meanwhile, think hard about what we can do to get out of this mess."

As a dirty pair of shoes appeared at the top of the ladder, Max and Sam lay still with their eyes shut. The man climbed down the ladder, turned on the cabin light, and banged around in the galley for several minutes before going back up to the deck.

Max and Sam sighed with relief. They were happy to be alone again.

CRASH—BAM—they heard coming from above as glass bottles were smashed on the deck.

"Pirates are the rowdiest beings on earth," Sam whispered to Max.

"I thought pirates were a thing of the past," Max whispered back.

"These creeps certainly *act* like pirates," Sam said in a hushed voice. "And they rob at sea like pirates—that's for sure. Even though they're not dressed like Captain Hook, they're modern-day pirates in my book." Sam covered his ears as the noise above them continued.

"He must be brewing tea on the stove," Max

whispered, breathing in the distinctive aroma.

From the sound of the noise above, the men showed no sign of calming down. Seeing their chance, Max and Sam dashed over to the galley to look for some food. Max opened a drawer and was just about to close it when Sam stopped him.

Sam picked up a box of sea-sickness pills and stared at them. A smile filled his face.

As Max continued with his search for food, Sam opened the new box of pills and snapped all of the pills out of their foil casing. He threw them in the pot and watched as the white dots sank into the simmering brown liquid and disappeared.

"What are you doing?" Max shrieked. "The only thing those pills will do is keep the men from getting sick."

"No way," Sam answered. "One time, a single pill knocked me out for an entire afternoon. They should label them as sleeping pills instead of sea-sickness pills because they make you so drowsy."

All at once, the noise dwindled and the boys rushed back over to take their places again.

"Time to have a midnight snack, mates," he heard a pirate bellow out. "There were some biscuits left over from dinner, and I've cooked up a tasty brew of tea!"

As the pirates stampeded down the stairs at the mention of food, Max and Sam closed their eyes tightly.

A pirate stopped in front of them and stared down. "Don't you think we should wake 'em to get some food in their bellies. We don't want 'em withering to nothing on us—we might have use for 'em."

"We'll wake 'em if we have any biscuits left over," one said. "Or better yet, we can wait till the morning to feed 'em some of that dead fish on the deck up above and make 'em clean the broken glass up."

"Good idea," another pirate said. "We don't want to give away any more of our grub than we have to."

Max and Sam silently cringed at the thought

of eating dead fish.

After stuffing themselves once again, the pirates sat around drinking their tea and reminiscing about old times.

One of them proudly told of how he had poked a grumpy, old man's eye out because he was rude to his bird. "I always wanted to be a pirate ever since I was a young boy, you see. So when I left my parent's house at the age of eighteen, the first thing I did was to buy myself a parrot. I worked for days teaching my parrot Do-Do how to talk," he explained. "That old man walked by and didn't even say hello to Do-Do when he said 'hi matey' for the very first time. You ought to have seen the sadness in my Do-Do's eyes."

The room grew more somber and the mood changed. "That's a bloody shame to treat a bird like that," one pirate said quietly after a few seconds. "That man got what he deserved."

"Hear, hear," a voice called out. "Let's drink to that."

They all raised their glasses clumsily to toast

the old man's punishment. The men appeared
to be in a stupor now, slurring their words and
moving in slow motion. Before long, there
were no words spoken at all. . . .

After a few minutes of silence, Max and Sam
glanced up at the men. They were amazed—six
overly stuffed, dirty pirates were sleeping like
babies, right before their eyes.

Max looked over at the clock that read one
o'clock. He got up and scurried over to look
out the porthole. . . .

He saw distant lights from scattered boats,
but the boats were too far away to help.

Max strained his eyes to the left to see if he
could spot land. He saw what appeared to be
trees and some twinkling of lights—it was too
dark to tell for sure.

Sam hovered beside him, trying to look out
the tiny round window. "I heard one of the men
say that he would go into port in the morning to
see about having the boat painted," Sam
recalled. "That must mean we're anchored by
land."

Chapter Eleven
The Forbidding Fort

S am gathered up rope from the numerous storage lockers about the boat. He then retrieved a long knife from the galley to cut the thick rope into long sections.

Max began to tie the first pirate's hands up. "Ooh, yuck," he groaned. "Look at his slimy, hairy hands. They look like they haven't been washed in years."

Sam looked up from his work and shuddered. "You think his *hands* are bad—look at his filthy, disgusting feet."

Max's eyes began to water at the strong stench coming from the pirate's body and clothes.

"How can they even stand to be around each other?" Max said, trying to breathe through his mouth and not his nose.

"Here," Sam said, handing him a mask and snorkel that were on the countertop. "Try this."

Max quickly put on the mask and snorkel. He began to breathe through the tube.

Sam looked over at him and chuckled. His face looked distorted and funny.

Even though the mask shielded Max from the smell, it did nothing to take away the oily feel of the skin as he worked to bind each pirate's ankles and wrists.

Sam followed after Max, tying each one's ankles and wrists with a second piece of rope.

Satisfied they had restrained their unwelcome guests, Max and Sam grabbed some bottles of water and snacks from the galley along with their raincoats and threw them in a bag.

They hurried up to the dimly lit deck, shutting the hatch behind them.

Sam quickly grabbed the hatch key from the ring of keys that was in the boat's ignition and locked the unsavory men in the cabin. He put the keys in his pocket.

"Let's hurry," Max said, as he raced over to hoist the dinghy. Both of the boys grabbed onto the rope and pulled with all their might. Finally, the dinghy was raised above the deck. They

tied the rope onto a cleat so that it wouldn't unwind. The boys then pushed the dinghy over to the side until it dangled over the water.

Sam quickly untied the rope, and the small lifeboat dropped to the water. Max held onto the guide rope so it wouldn't drift away.

Sam climbed inside the little vinyl boat and tossed their supply bag on the floor. He held onto the side of the railing of the big boat until Max got safely inside.

Max nervously eyed *The Strong Survivor* and turned to his brother. "Are you sure they won't be able to break free?"

"If they do, it'll take them a while," Sam said, deep in thought. "We tied every pirate's wrists and ankles *two* times, and I locked them in the cabin just in case they *do* get loose. The lights in the cabin are off, so if they wake up in the night, it'll be harder for them to see what they're doing."

Satisfied, Max nodded his head and pushed off the side of the sailboat with both of his hands. The dinghy drifted away.

Through the dark water, Max and Sam began to row vigorously toward the cluster of lights and trees. Everything seemed frightening in the black of the night.

As they grew closer to land, they spotted a huge fort lit up and sprawled out on a hill. It looked like something out of a history book with its stone buildings and look-out towers.

"What in the world is *that*?" Sam said, pointing to the medieval fort on the hill.

"That's the Fort of El Morro!" Max said excitedly, as he continued to row. "I saw a pic-

ture of it in a book about Puerto Rico. Dad went there on a trip."

"It looks pretty scary," Sam said as he stared up at the forbidding six-level castle fortress. "I'm not sure I want to go there."

"It will be a great place to hide until morning," Max said. "We can look down on the water and see if the pirates are coming."

"Can't we track down the police or something *tonight*?" Sam said, as they reached the shore.

Max looked up at the fort in front of them. "I don't see anybody around," he said. He noticed a cemetery beside the fort and shivered. "I'm not sure I want to stay here either—it looks really scary—but I'm not sure I want to walk through the streets of the city in the middle of the night either. That might even be *worse*."

"Let's go then," Sam said, getting out of the dinghy. He waited for Max to get out before pulling the tiny boat out of the water.

As the boys bravely headed up the hill toward the fort, the waves lapped gently on the shore behind them. A cool, salty breeze ruffled the leaves of the palm trees up ahead.

Max and Sam couldn't take their eyes off of the fort as they walked. It loomed proudly on the hill—looking every bit as intimidating as it was meant to look when it was built over four hundred years ago.

When they reached it, they climbed over its wall and started to walk through its dimly lit maze of tunnels. They walked slowly until they spotted some stairs. As they made their way down the dark stairs, a musty smell overwhelmed them. At the bottom of the stairs was a room that appeared to be a dungeon. It was hard to make out much of what was there because the only light came from a sconce on the wall outside the opening of the room.

Suddenly, chills went down their spines. They could hear a voice calling out their names. The voice echoed through the stone wall corridors of the fort.

Max and Sam panicked, thinking it could be one of the pirates. They didn't want to get trapped in the dungeon so they bolted up the stairs and back through the tunnel, running aimlessly through the dark fort. They ran until they spotted a chapel at the end of the way.

They hurried into the dark sanctuary, slipped behind a pew, and waited. . . .

After several minutes, the door creaked open, and they heard footsteps. The steps walked around the room before stopping in front of them. Max and Sam could see the shadowy figure of a man on the wall, as light streamed in from one of the arched windows.

Suddenly, a phone rang. They heard a familiar voice speak into the receiver. "Hello," the man said. "Yes, I'm still searching for them. So far, there's no sign of them."

"Dad!" Max and Sam shouted as they barreled out from behind the pew, almost knocking Mr. Stone to the ground.

"How did you find us?" Max blurted out, giving him a hug.

Mr. Stone was so overjoyed at the sight of his boys, he let his phone fall to the ground and scooped them up in his arms to hold them close. Tears of happiness streamed down his face.

"It wasn't easy," their dad finally answered, choking back more tears. "After I got my hands untied, I sailed to the nearest port. After a lot of red tape, I finally got the authorities to send out a helicopter to look for you. When they located your boat, they stormed it and found six tied-up men—all sound asleep—and no sign of you. The dinghy was missing, and so we knew you must have come to shore."

Max and Sam smiled at their dad. They should have known he would break free to rescue them.

"Don't worry," Mr. Stone said. "The pirates are in custody now—right where they belong."

"Are we going back to the boat to sleep?" Sam asked leerily.

"I think we've had enough of the sea for now," Mr. Stone said, laughing. "Let's splurge on a fancy hotel room."

"I was hoping you'd say that," Max said. "I think I've had enough of the sea for a *lifetime*."

Facts About the Virgin Islands

~The Virgin Islands are two groups of islands in the Caribbean Sea, east of Puerto Rico, that are divided into two territories: the United States Virgin Islands and the British Virgin Islands.

~The U.S. Virgin Islands territory is made up of St. Croix, St. Thomas, St. John, and Water Island, along with a number of smaller islands.

~The British Virgin Islands territory, or BVI, is made up of 16 inhabited Caribbean islands. The largest ones are Tortola, Virgin Gorda, Jost Van Dyke, and Anegada. There are many other islands in the BVI that are uninhabited.

~Both the U. S. and British Virgin Islands use the U. S. dollar as their currency and English as their official language.

~In both territories, drivers drive on the left side of the road.

~The people of the U.S. Virgin Islands are American citizens, but are unable to vote in federal elections.

~The BVI is a British overseas territory.

Facts About Puerto Rico

Population: almost four million
Currency: U. S. dollar
Language: Spanish
Capital: San Juan

~Puerto Rico is an island in the Caribbean that is approximately one hundred miles long and thirty-five miles wide. It is about the size of the state of Connecticut and is the smallest and the most eastern island of the Greater Antilles.

~Puerto Rico was discovered in 1493 by Christopher Columbus and was a Spanish colony for four centuries. As a result of the Spanish-American War, Puerto Rico was relinquished to the United States by Spain in 1898. Today it is a self-governing territory of the United States and is known as the Commonwealth of Puerto Rico.

~Puerto Rico has waterfalls, beaches, mountains, and rain forests. The tropical climate is warm, staying around 80 degrees year-round.

~The Fort of El Morro, at the tip of Old San Juan, was built between 1540-1783 to prevent seaborne enemies from conquering the island of Puerto Rico.

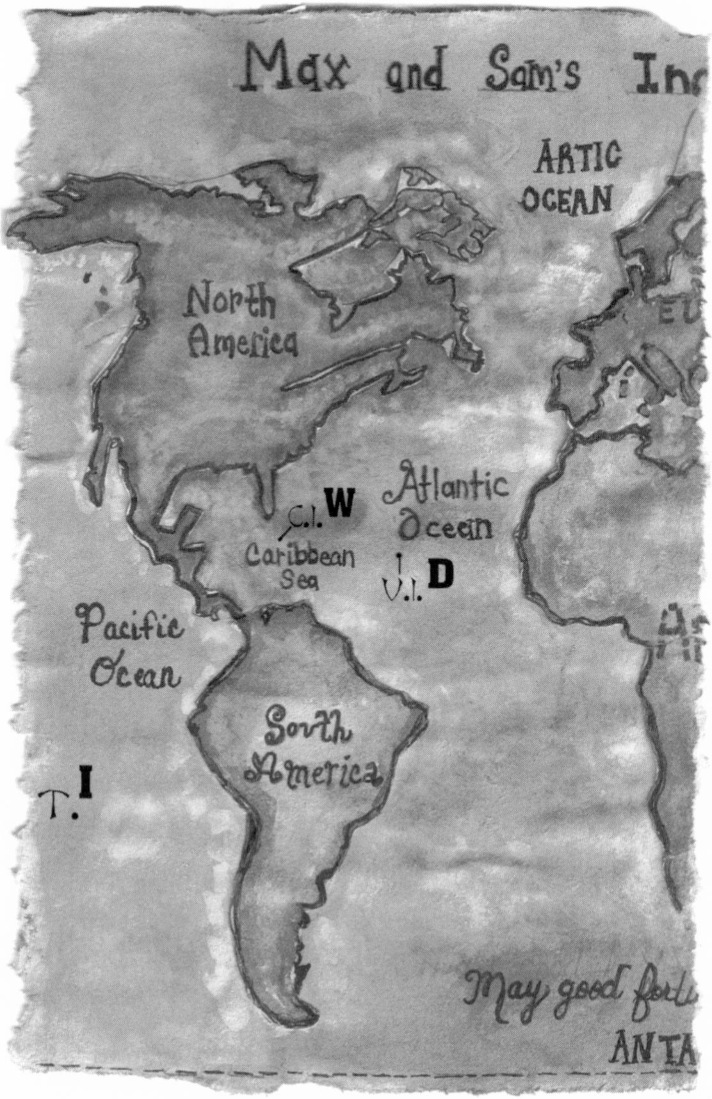

Max and Sam's In
ARTIC OCEAN
North America
Atlantic Ocean
W
C.I.
Caribbean Sea
D
V.I.
Pacific Ocean
South America
T.
I
May good fort
ANTA

redible Journey Map
ROPE
Asia
Sea of Japan
South China Sea
Pacific Ocean
S
FRICA
Indian Ocean
N
W
E
S
Australia
me be with you
RCTICA
Oct. 11, 1964

MAX AND SAM'S SCIENCE PICK
Ocean in a Bottle

Steps to create your own waves:

1. Take a two-liter plastic bottle with a cap and remove its label; wash inside of the bottle.
2. Fill the bottle halfway with water.
3. Add three to four drops of blue food coloring and mix.
4. Decorate by adding glitter, small plastic fish, and shells.
5. Using a funnel, fill the bottle with vegetable oil, almost to the top.
6. Dry the rim and cap; apply glue to the rim and twist on the cap to seal.
7. Turn the bottle on its side and gently rock the bottle to produce waves.

Why the mixture creates waves:

The vegetable oil is less dense than water, so the oil floats. The two will never mix.

NOW THAT'S COOL SCIENCE!